For Emil, Ben & Ralph A.C.

For Oliver with love D.R.

First published 2020 by Walker Books Ltd, 87 Vauxhall Walk, London SE11 5HJ

This edition published 2021

2 4 6 8 10 9 7 5 3 1

Text © 2020 Alastair Chisholm • Illustrations © 2020 David Roberts

This book has been typeset in AnkeSans

Printed in China

British Library Cataloguing in Publication Data: a catalogue record for
this book is available from the British Library

ISBN 978-1-4063-6281-7

www.walker.co.uk

WALKER BOOKS
AND SUBSIDIARIES
LONDON • BOSTON • SYDNEY • AUCKLAND

INCH AND GRUB

A STORY ABOUT CAVEMEN

Alastair Chisholm   illustrated by David Roberts

This is **Inch**.

This is **Grub**.

Inch and Grub were cavemen. Inch and Grub lived in caves.

Inch's cave was nice, but Grub's cave was **bigger**.

"Me have **bigger** cave than you," said Grub. "That make me the best."

This made Inch cross. "That not fair!" he said.

"Look," said Inch. "Me have cave with **water** now. **Me** am best!"

But Grub rubbed two sticks together and made ...

FIRE.

"Ooooooo!" said Inch.

"Well, you silly caveman, sitting on ground," said Inch. "Me have made a chair."

"Only chair?" sniffed Grub. "Me have made BED!"

"Me have bed too! And walls. Me have a house!" said Inch.

"Pah!" said Grub. "Me am built castle. Me am LORD Grub!"

"Me have bigger castle!
Me have castle and
tower!" said Inch.
"Me am King Inch,
and you bow now!"

"Hmmph," muttered Grub.

"Me have discovered **horses**," said Grub proudly. "Me can ride horse very fast!"

"Me have horse and carriage," said Inch.

"Carriages old and silly," scoffed Grub.
"Me have made TRAIN. You have train?"

"No," said Inch...

"Me have CAR! Ha ha, me go *VROOM! VROOM! VROOM!*"

Grub stamped his foot crossly.

"And me have shiny buildings," said Inch. "Me have **skyscrapers**. Very tall!"

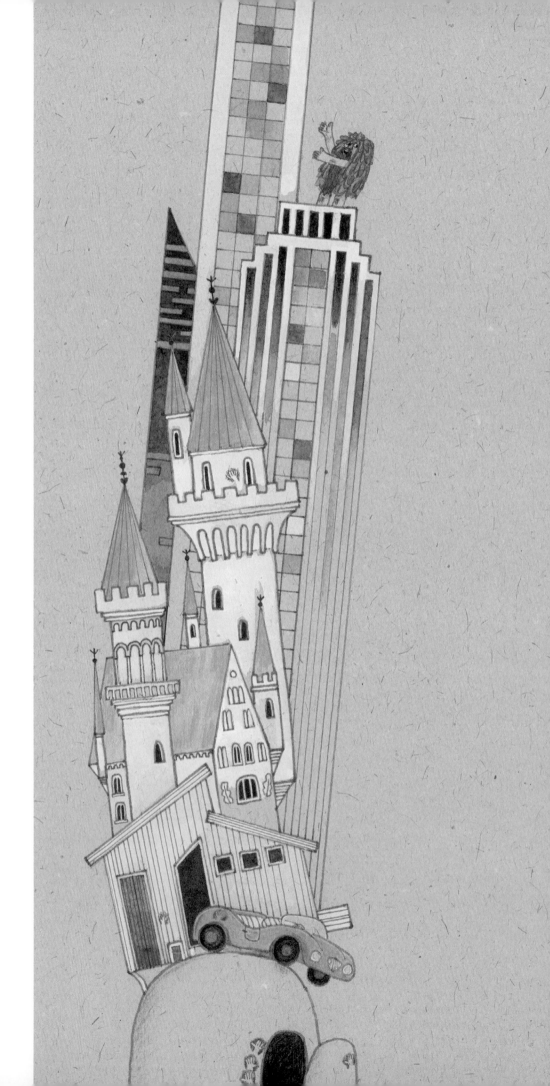

"Me have fancy boat!"
said Grub.

"And me have radio!"

"Me can't talk to you now, me am on the PHONE," said Inch.

"Me have a plane,

Woosh!"

shouted Grub.

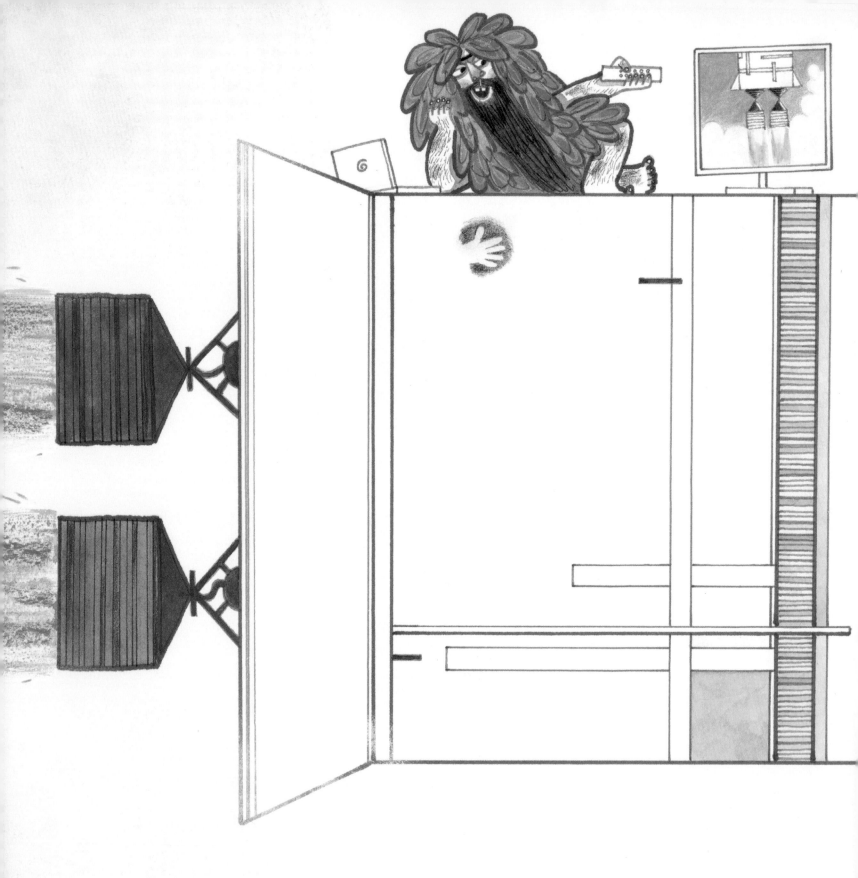

"Me have **rocket**," crowed Inch. "And **computer**!
And ... **television**."

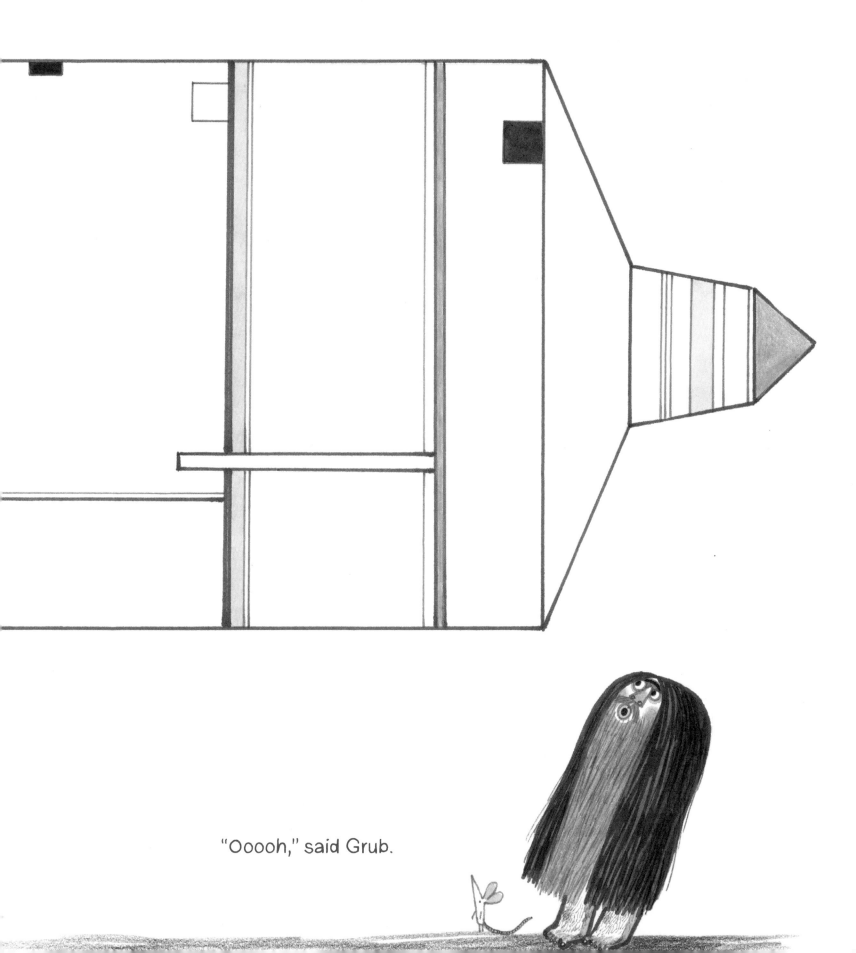

"Ooooh," said Grub.

And on they went, collecting more stuff, and forgetting all about their lovely old caves.

Satellites and statuettes and submarines and super-jets — until one day...

"Me have silver-plated drinking straw!" said Inch, and he placed it on the top of his tall, tall pile of Things.

"Me have gold-plated drinking straw!" said Grub, and placed it on *his* tall, tall pile.

The piles ... started to wobble.

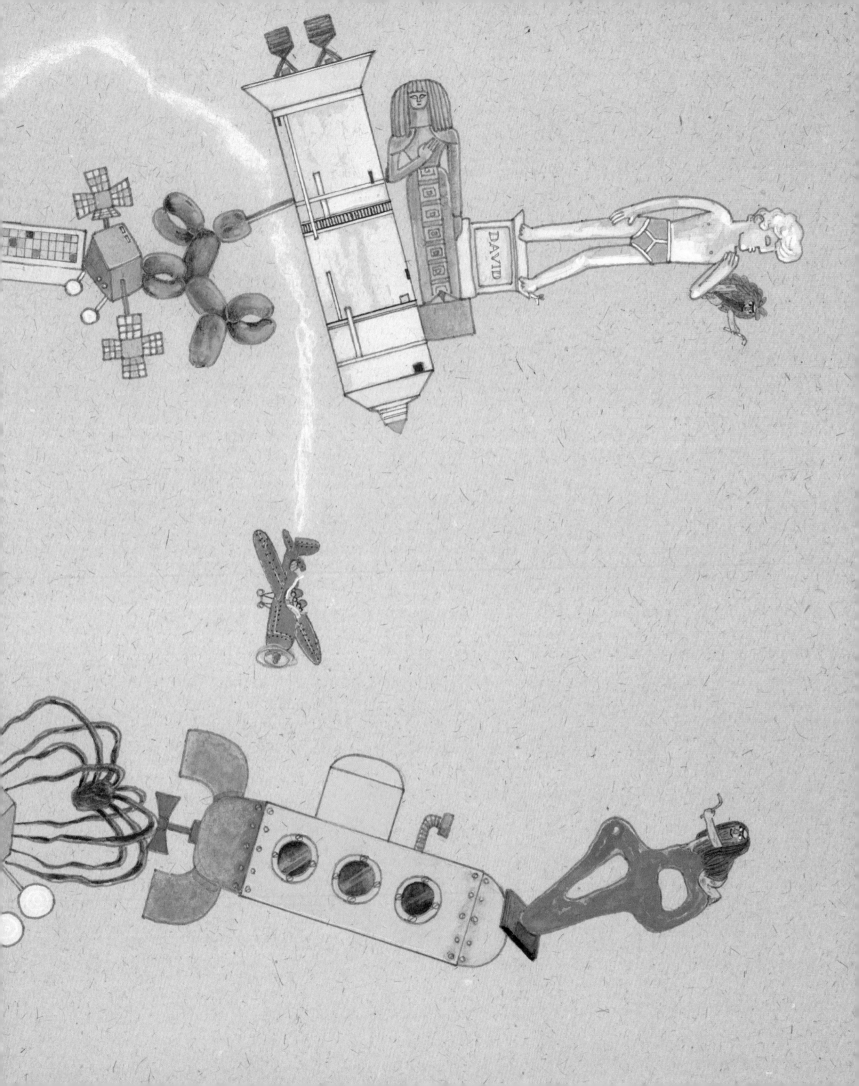

"Ha ha!" sneered Inch. "Your pile is wobbling!"

"Ha ha!" sneered Grub. "Your pile is wobbling!"

"Oh-oh," said Inch and Grub.

Down crashed the piles!

Down fell the straws!

Down came the castles

and boats

and buildings

and rockets

and radios!

Crash!

Bang!

All down on Inch and Grub!

"Owwwww," said Inch,
 holding his head.

"Owwwww," said Grub.

Inch looked around.

"All me have left is dust," he said sadly. "Me think me was better in cave."

"Me too," said Grub.

"This am all YOUR fault!" shouted Inch.

"No!" shouted Grub. "This am all YOUR—"
He stopped.

"This ..." he said slowly, "am all ... OUR fault."

Grub looked at Inch.

Inch looked at Grub.

Inch thought really hard.

"Me have ... a rock," he said at last. "You want ... share ... rock?"

"... Yeah," said Grub.

And they sat on the rock together.

THE END

Me am **Alastair Chisholm**. Me write books.
Me am write sci-fi adventure *Orion Lost*.
Me am also write picture books *The Prince and the Witch
and the Thief and the Bears* and *The Tale of the Valiant Ninja Frog*.
Me live in Edinburgh.

Me am **David Roberts**. Me draw books.
Me draw picture books *Rosie Revere, Engineer, Ada Twist, Scientist,
The Dunderheads, His Royal Tinyness* and lots others.
Me write and draw non-fiction book *Suffragette: The Battle for Equality*.
Me live in London.